P9-DXF-817

This book belongs to:

. . . .

Christmas Cheer

For Cas, Jim, Sarah, Thomas, Chelsea,
Madeline & Joshua Wickenden
—S. G.

First published in Great Britain by Bloomsbury Publishing Plc
Published in the United States by Bloomsbury U.S.A. Children's Books
175 Fifth Avenue, New York, New York 10010

Library of Congress Cataloging-in-Publication Data
Grindley, Sally.
Christmas cheer : a collection of holiday tales / by Sally Grindley. — 1st U.S. ed.
v.   cm.
Summary: A collection of eight new or retold stories, illustrated by various artists,
which feature such things as an ill reindeer, an elf who gets locked in the workshop,
and a boy who cannot decide what he wants Santa Claus to bring.
ISBN-13: 978-1-59990-188-6 • ISBN-10: 1-59990-188-9
1. Jesus Christ—Nativity—Juvenile fiction. 2. Christmas stories, American. 3. Children's stories, American.
[1. Jesus Christ—Nativity—Fiction. 2. Christmas—Fiction. 3. Short stories.] I. Title.
PZ7.G88446Chr 2008   [E]—dc22   2008007426

First U.S. Edition 2008
Printed in China
2 4 6 8 10 9 7 5 3 1

All papers used by Bloomsbury U.S.A. are natural, recyclable products
made from wood grown in well-managed forests. The manufacturing processes
conform to the environmental regulations of the country of origin.

Christmas Cheer

A COLLECTION OF HOLIDAY TALES

Sally Grindley

BLOOMSBURY
CHILDREN'S
BOOKS

CONTENTS

The Reluctant Fairy

When Priscilla was told that she was going to be a Christmas tree fairy, she was very unhappy.

"I don't want to sit amongst a load of prickles for the whole of Christmas," she grumbled. "Why can't I be a flower fairy or a sugar plum fairy?"

"Everyone has to take their turn," said the Queen of the Fairies.

Priscilla stuck out her tongue when the Queen of the Fairies wasn't looking, but she had to do as she was told.

She was taken to a shop and put on a shelf full of Christmas tree fairies. She tried to make herself look as ugly as possible so that nobody would want her, then perhaps she would be sent back home. It didn't work. A little girl came into the shop and pointed to her straight away.

"That one, Mummy," the little girl said. "Can we have the one with the bright red dress?"

"Her face isn't very pretty," the girl's mother said, much to Priscilla's annoyance, but the girl pleaded until her mother gave in.

The little girl skipped all the way home with Priscilla in her hands. She played with her, stretching her legs this way and that, bending her in half and twizzling her head from side to side. Priscilla gave her her worst glare and was relieved when the little girl dropped her on to a chair and ran to help her mother and her brothers decorate the tree. By the time the tree was ready for its fairy, Priscilla was

glad to be placed on top, out of the girl's reach.

"There," said the girl's mother. "All finished. It's a pity that fairy looks so grumpy."

"She'll look happy on Christmas Day," said the little girl.

As soon as they had gone out of the room, Priscilla stretched her wings and shook her legs. "I bet they'd look

grumpy if they were in my place," she grumbled. She looked down through the branches of the tree at the brightly coloured baubles and golden tinsel. "If only I could untie myself, I could have some fun with those," she thought to herself. She pulled at the string then wriggled from side to side. The string felt looser. She wriggled again and it dropped from round her waist to round her knees. "That was easy," she smiled. She twisted this way and that. The string dropped down to her feet. She quickly grabbed hold of a branch because nothing was holding her any more. "Easy-peasy," she grinned. "Watch out baubles, here I come!"

Priscilla scrambled carefully from branch to branch. Every time she reached a bauble she sat on it and rocked backwards and forwards. "Whee!" she cried. She clambered down to a snowman covered in silver foil

and discovered that it was chocolate inside. She took a big bite. "Yummy," she said. She stood next to a glass angel holding a sheet of music and pretended to sing with her. "La, la, la," she sang. She came to a plastic model of Father Christmas in his sleigh and jumped in next to him. "Giddy-up, Rudolph," she yelled.

She was just about to leap on to a flying swan, when she heard a loud THUMP! A cloud of black smoke filled the room. "HO, HO, HO!" a voice boomed. "Mince pies, my favourite!"

"It's Santa!" Priscilla squealed. She was so shocked she couldn't move.

"Did I hear a mouse?" she heard Santa say. A shadow fell across her and a very large finger prodded her shoulder. "Who's this next to me in my sleigh?" he chuckled.

Priscilla looked up into his beaming face.

"Shouldn't you be on the top of the tree?" he asked.

"I was just exploring," said Priscilla nervously.

"Ah, yes, exploring," said Santa. "Something I've done

a lot of in my time. How would you like to help me fill these stockings?"

Priscilla looked to where Santa was pointing. Five stockings were hanging from the mantelpiece. "Yes, please!" she cried, and nearly fell out of the tree again.

"You can put the chocolate gold coins in," he said. "They're not too heavy." He lifted her to the floor and she followed him to his sack.

Priscilla couldn't believe her luck. She dived into the sack over and over again and helped Santa to pull out pencils and pens and toy soldiers and dolls and farm animals and tiny teddies and rings and bracelets. As soon as she found the gold coins she flew with them one by one up to the mantelpiece and dropped them carefully into the stockings. When they were finished, Santa invited her to sit down and enjoy his mince pies with him before he set off again.

"Now, my little helper, what would you like for yourself?" he said.

Priscilla thought and said, "More than anything else I would like a magic wand."

"Then you shall have one," said Santa. He delved around in his sack until at last he pulled out a golden wand with a shiny silver star. "Hey presto!" he boomed. He put the wand into Priscilla's hand and lifted her up to the top of the tree. In a flash he was gone.

Priscilla smiled to herself at all the magic she could perform when nobody was looking, then she fell fast asleep. She was woken the next morning by the astonished cries of the little girl. "Mummy," she heard, "our fairy's got a magic wand!"

"Well I never!" exclaimed the mother. "How on earth did that get there?"

"Perhaps Santa gave it to her," said the little girl.

"Perhaps he did," said the mother. "And our fairy certainly looks happier now it's Christmas Day."

"And so would you," Priscilla smiled to herself, "if you were a Christmas tree fairy."

Good News

One very cold, frosty night, a flock of sheep huddled together in the corner of a field. Most of them were dozing quietly. The smallest of them was wide awake and looking at the sky. An incredibly bright star had appeared, its light shining down on a place far in the distance.

"I've never seen a star do that before," the smallest sheep said to herself. She nudged the sheep standing next to her.

"Baaa," complained the sheep. "Why are you waking me up?"

"There's a really bright star up there," said the smallest sheep. "What do you suppose it means?"

"It means you've made me cross for waking me up," bleated the sheep. She shuffled away and hid behind the rest of the flock.

The smallest sheep stared at the sky again then prodded the sheep standing closest to her.

"Ba-a-a-a-a," quaked the sheep. "Is there a wolf coming?"

"There's an amazingly bright star in the sky. What do you think it means?"

"It means you frightened the life out of me," snorted the sheep.

She scampered away and hid in the middle of the flock.

The smallest sheep asked one sheep after another to look at the star, but none of them cared what it meant. It was night-time and night-time meant sleep-time. The smallest sheep was determined to find out where the light from the star was falling. If none of the other sheep would go with her, then she would go on her own.

She set off across the field. By the time she had reached the edge she already felt very lonely, but she looked up at the sky and kept on going. She scampered along a muddy path which led to some woods. She was scared to go through the woods in case there were wolves inside, but there was no other way so she kept on going. She reached the other side and looked up at the sky again. The star seemed to be shining even more brightly, but she still had a long way to go before she would reach the place where its light was falling. The path ahead was overhung with trees, making it even darker and more frightening than the woods. The smallest sheep wondered if she should go

home, but she had a feeling that something extraordinary was happening that night and she wanted to be part of it. She started to walk faster. "I'm not scared," she kept saying to herself. "I am going on a journey and it will have a happy ending." She made herself think about nothing else except reaching the light at the end of her journey. Even when she heard noises in the undergrowth she kept on walking. Even when she heard wolves howling, she refused to turn back. Even when her legs were so tired that she could barely put one in front of the other, she would not give up. Every so often she would look up, see the star and press determinedly onwards.

At last she came to a town. She had never been to a town before. She wandered along one street after another, trying to avoid the hundreds of human feet that were hurrying up and down. Then suddenly everyone seemed to be going in the same direction. She went with them, carried along by the sense of excitement. When they stopped at last,

she pushed her way through their legs to reach the front. She found herself in a stable. In the middle of the stable was a little wooden trough. The smallest sheep was astonished to see that the light from the star fell straight on to the face of a tiny baby lying in the trough. "What's a baby doing in a trough?" she asked herself.

She gazed around. There were other animals standing near the trough. There were shepherds kneeling down and a man and woman were sitting beside it. Everyone looked so happy that it made the smallest sheep feel happy too.

"It's good news, isn't it?" a donkey whispered to her.

The smallest sheep nodded but didn't know what he meant.

"It's amazing that a baby is going to save us," the donkey continued.

"What's he going to save us from?" asked the smallest sheep.

"Bad things, I expect," said the donkey.

"Like wolves?" asked the smallest sheep.

The donkey nodded. "He's going to make the world a better place."

"That baby must be very special," said the

smallest sheep. "Can I tell my family and friends about him?"

"Tell everyone about him," said the donkey. "Everyone likes to hear good news."

So that's just what the smallest sheep did.

Dear Santa

Dear Santa

G*eorge* picked up his big blue writing pad and his pen with a bear on top. "Dear Santa," he wrote, "for Christmas I think I would like a train set. I have been quite good so I hope that will be all right." He folded the paper in half. "I've written my letter to Santa, Mummy," he called. "Can we post it now?"

He skipped along beside her as they went to the postbox. On the way back home again, George saw a boy on a scooter. "I wish I had one of those," he said to his mother.

"Christmas is coming," she replied.

"But I've already asked for a train set," said George.

"Which would you prefer?" she asked.

"A scooter I think," said George.

"Then you'd better write another letter to Santa," she smiled.

When they arrived back home, George took his big blue writing pad and his pen with a bear on top and wrote, "Dear Santa, I'm sorry but I've changed my mind. I'd like a scooter for Christmas, though I still like train sets. I've been quite good so I hope that will be all right. Love, George."

After they'd been to the postbox again, George sat down to watch his favourite programme on the television. It was a wildlife programme all about elephants. George got very excited when a huge bull elephant charged through the trees. "Did you see that, Mummy?" he cried. When a baby elephant stood underneath its mother he couldn't help laughing. "I love elephants," he said. "I wish I could have one."

"A real one?!" laughed his mother.

"Not a real one," laughed George. "It wouldn't fit in our garden! I mean a furry one that can sit on my bed."

"Christmas is coming," his mother replied.

"But I've already asked for a train set and a scooter."

"Which do you want the most?"

"A cuddly elephant, I think," said George.

"Then you'd better write another letter," said his mother. "Poor Santa, he'll be very confused."

George took his big blue writing pad and his pen with a bear on top and wrote, "Dear Santa, It's me, George, again. I'm sorry to be a pest but I think what I really want for Christmas is a cuddly elephant instead of a train set and scooter. I've been quite good so I hope that will be all right. I hope you're not confused. Love, George."

It was too late to go out again that night, so they went to the postbox the next morning. On the way home, George saw a little yellow bike in a shop window. "Look at that bike," he said to his mother. "I'd like to have a bike like that."

"More than an elephant?" asked his mother.

George thought for a moment. "An elephant would be nice to have in bed, but I could ride a bike round the garden and to the postbox."

"You could carry your elephant to the postbox," smiled his mother.

"In a basket on the back of my bike," giggled George.

"Well, I don't know that Santa will bring you both," said his mother, "so you'll have to choose."

"A bike," said George.

"Another letter?" grinned his mother.

"Do you think Santa will mind?" asked George.

"I think my feet will protest if they go to the postbox many more times," said his mother.

George took his big blue writing pad and his pen with a bear on top. "This will be my last letter," he said, "because it's my last piece of writing paper."

And then he wrote, "Dear Santa, You know I told you I wanted a train set and a scooter and an elephant? Well, I've seen a little yellow bike and I think I would like that more than anything, if it's not too much trouble. I'm sorry I keep changing my mind. Mum's got sore feet so I won't change it again. I've been quite good so I hope that will be all right. Love, George." Just as he finished, his pen with the bear on top ran out of ink.

"Definitely no more letters then," said his mother.

"No more letters," said George.

George couldn't wait for Christmas to arrive. When at last it did, he rushed into the room to see what was under the tree. He could see a bike-shaped present amongst all the other presents. "Do you think that's my bike?" he said excitedly to his mother.

"Open it and have a look," she said.

He opened it and there was the little yellow bike.

"Thank you, thank you, Santa," he said. Then he opened his other presents. He couldn't believe his eyes when he found a big fluffy elephant and a wooden train set. "Santa gave me three of the things I asked for," he cried.

"That must be because you've been very good," said his mother.

"There's still one more to open," said George, "but it doesn't look like a scooter." He tore off the paper. Inside he found a big blue writing pad and a pen with an elephant on top. "How did Santa know?" he said in amazement.

"I think he must have guessed," laughed his mother.

"Now I can write him a thank you letter," said George. And that's just what he did, then he cycled to the postbox on his little yellow bike with his big fluffy elephant on the back.

The Enormous Cake

Mrs Ball decided to make a cake for Christmas. She had never made a cake before, in fact, she was not a very good cook, but she wanted to surprise her family. She opened a recipe book and searched for cakes. When she found a recipe she liked, she listed all the ingredients she would need.

"If I am to feed my six children and my husband and my

mother and my sister and her husband, I shall need to make my cake four times as big as the one in the book," she said to herself. "That means four times as much of each of the ingredients."

Mrs Ball took her list and went off to the shops. When she returned she was carrying two enormous shopping bags. She emptied them out, then searched her cupboards for the biggest baking tin she could find. "This will have to do," she said, placing a large tin on the table. She took out her measuring cups and began to measure the ingredients in turn. There were raisins and currants and cherries and apricots and nuts and candied peel. There was butter and eggs and milk and flour and baking powder, which makes cakes rise. Every time she came to a new ingredient, Mrs Ball tried to remember that she needed four

times as much as the recipe said. Soon her mixing bowl was so full that she had to leave some on the table and mix it there.

When it was time to add the baking powder, Mrs Ball put in six times as much. "I want my cake to be the biggest my children have ever seen," she smiled, and then added an extra spoonful of the powder for good luck. The pile of cake mixture was now so huge that it wouldn't fit in the tin. "I'll have to put it on a baking tray," said Mrs Ball. She took one, tipped the mixture on to it, and put it into the hot oven. "It'll be ready in three hours. That'll give me time to have a nice cup of tea and a little doze. I'm quite exhausted."

She sat down in a chair with a cup of tea and was soon asleep. When she woke two hours later, she jumped up to see how her cake was progressing. To her horror, she discovered that it was already touching the top and the sides of the oven. Even as she looked at it, it seemed to grow larger. "Oh my goodness me," she cried. "I'd better

take it out before it explodes." She put on her oven gloves, grabbed the tray and pulled it out on to the table. In front of her very eyes, the cake spread across the table and rose towards the ceiling.

Just then Mrs Ball's six children arrived home from school. "What's cooking, Mum?" they called. When they walked into the kitchen, they stopped in their tracks and stared.

"What's that?" asked Jonny.

"It's a cake," said Mrs Ball.

"It's big," said Jimmy.

"It's huge," giggled Jenny.

"It's growing," laughed Jeanie.

"It's nearly reached the light bulb," hooted Jamie.

"It's eaten the light bulb," shrieked Janny.

"We'd better take it outside before it knocks the house down," cried Mrs Ball.

They lifted the table and shuffled to the door. The cake was so wide and so tall that it only just went through the gap. As soon as they put it down in the garden, it spread even further, until Mrs Ball said that they would have to move it again before it knocked down the garden fence. She asked her neighbours to help, and between them they lifted it on to the village green.

News travelled fast about the enormous cake. All the villagers left their houses and gathered round to watch it ballooning. It wasn't until the cake completely covered the

village green that it stopped growing. Mrs Ball breathed a huge sigh of relief. She had been scared that it would swallow the whole village. The children began to dance around it, while the adults discussed what should be done with it.

"As far as I can see," said the Mayor, "there's only one thing to be done with it."

"What's that?" asked Mrs Ball nervously.

"With your permission," smiled the Mayor, "we must eat it."

So that's what happened. On Christmas Day, all the villagers gathered round the village green, plate and spoon in hand, and helped themselves to as much cake as they could possibly eat. When they had had enough, they allowed all the hens, cats, dogs, pigs, goats and other animals to have their fill. It was left to the birds to finish off the last few crumbs. As for Mrs Ball, she was over the moon because everyone agreed that her cake was the best cake ever.

Almost Perfect

When the door slammed shut, Elmer woke up. He rubbed his eyes, stood up too quickly and banged his head. He began to panic. What time was it? How long had he been asleep? Why was it so quiet? He crept out from under the conveyor belt and looked around. The factory was empty. All the other elves had gone. He ran to the door and rattled the handle. It was locked. He ran to a window and tried to open it. It was locked as well, and anyway it was too high to jump from.

"I don't believe it!" he cried. "It's Christmas Eve and I'm stuck in the factory!"

The elves looked forward to Christmas Eve. After days and days spent making toys, they held a huge party. They had balloons and confetti, noisemakers and streamers, jellies and ice creams, chocolates and candies.

They hopped and skipped and jumped and jigged. They chanted and chorused and yodelled and sang. And then they let off fireworks that filled the sky with multi-coloured stars.

Elmer groaned with dismay. "It's the best day of the year, and I'm going to miss it." He walked round the factory kicking at empty boxes.

The toys had been wrapped up, labelled, and packed on to Santa's sleigh. The only toys that were left were those

 that had something wrong with them. These were piled high in waste bins. Elmer pulled out a teddy with one ear and a doll with one leg. "Poor things," he said. "You're going to miss Christmas as well, but at least I haven't got anything wrong with me." And then he had an idea. If he was going to be stuck in the factory all night long, he might as well make himself useful.

He rushed to the cupboards that lined the walls and opened them. He pulled out a box filled with scraps of fur, pieces of cotton, buttons, needles and pins. He took another that was crammed with eyes and noses, legs and arms. In a third box he found plastic, wire, gold and silver. "Perfect!" he said as he tipped them all out on to a table.

He picked up the bear with one ear and looked through the scraps of fur. "We'll begin with you" he said.

For the next few hours, Elmer

stitched and hammered and glued and painted. When at last he had finished, his fingers were sore and he could hardly keep his eyes open. "There," he said, "now you can enjoy Christmas too." He lined all the toys up along the conveyor belt and admired his work. The bear had a second ear, made of not quite the same sort of fur but close enough. The doll had a second leg, a little bit too long but at least she could stand up. The train had a new bell (which clanked rather than rang), the fairy's wing was mended (though it was still bent), the dinosaur had a roar (well, it was more like a squeak), and the fireman had two eyes (even if they were different colours).

There were lots of other toys too, none of them perfect but all of them complete.

Elmer was so tired that he crept back under the conveyor belt and fell fast asleep. He was woken again by a strange light and the sound of music. For a moment he didn't know where he was, and then he thought perhaps the

other elves had returned. He crawled out from under the conveyor belt. What he saw made him rub his eyes in astonishment.

Moonlight shone through the window on to a magical wonderland. The toys he had made good had come to life! In one corner the teddy bears were having a huge picnic. In another, the dolls were having a tea party. The train was steaming round and round the conveyor belt, its carriages full of toy passengers, its bell clanking loudly.

The dinosaurs were running races with horses, pigs, sheep and cows, all of them making a tremendous racket. The fireman and a policeman stood at the start and finishing lines ready to blow their whistles. Meanwhile, up above them all, close to the ceiling, a crowd of fairies sang songs.

As soon as they saw Elmer, the toys all cheered and thanked him for making them complete. One by one they invited him to join in with the fun, and for the next few hours that's exactly what he did.

Until the light from the moon disappeared, and everything fell still.

When the elves came into the factory the next morning, full of stories about their wonderful Christmas Eve, they were shocked to discover that Elmer had been shut there all night.

"You missed all the fun," they cried.

"I had plenty of fun myself," said Elmer. "And I've learned that you shouldn't throw things away just because they're not perfect."

From a sack under the conveyor belt, Elmer thought he heard a giggle, but he couldn't be sure. It was full of the toys he had rescued, and he was going to take them home.

Snowy Snowy Night

Jo wanted it to snow for Christmas. Every morning for a week she jumped out of bed, ran to the window and looked out. It was always sunny or raining or just grey, grey, grey.

"Why won't it snow?" she said to her father.

"It hasn't snowed at Christmas for years," replied her father. "And it's not due to snow this year either."

On Christmas Eve Jo went to bed disappointed, even though she was excited about what Santa might bring her. "Tonight's the last chance for it to snow," she said to her father when he kissed her goodnight.

"I think your luck's out this time, Jojo," he smiled. "Anyway, if it snows Santa and his reindeer might slide off our roof."

Jo giggled and burrowed down under her covers. "I'm going to wish and wish and wish to make it snow," she said, shutting her eyes.

When she opened them again, the house was so quiet that she could hear her own breathing and her room was strangely light. "There must be a full moon," she whispered to herself. She jumped out of bed, ran to the window and pulled back the curtains. For a moment she was blinded. She rubbed her eyes and stared out again. Everywhere was white! The ground was covered with snow and the light from the moon made it glisten like diamonds. The trees were bowing and curtseying under the weight of snow. The roofs were mantled with deep velvety snow. Flakes of snow the size of golf balls were falling from the sky.

"Wow!" Jo exclaimed. She could scarcely tell where her garden ended and the village green began, the snow was so deep. The green appeared to be dotted with white shapes which seemed to glide first one way then the other. "Snowmen!" Jo gasped. Children were skating round them, marking out figures of eight and spinning perfect pirouettes. Others were racing along on toboggans, even though the ground was flat. When a group of penguins waddled over to Jo's garden looking as if they were deep in conversation, she laughed out loud.

Just then, a snowy owl flew up, tapped on her window with its beak, and signalled with its wing for her to go outside.

"Me?" Jo mouthed.

The owl nodded. Jo didn't need to be asked twice. She pulled on some warm clothes, ran down the stairs and out through the back door.

The cold air bit at her skin and the light hurt her eyes as she stepped into the garden. She was quickly swept up by the group of penguins who slithered and slid with her over to the green. There she was greeted by the other children, all of them happy to see her. They held up some skates for her to put on, which fitted perfectly. "Follow us," they cried. They set off round the green, chattering loudly, laughing and singing Christmas songs. Jo joined in with them as they danced round the snowmen, who lifted their hats and waggled their noses. She followed them as they leapt on to toboggans and headed off along the village streets. "We

wish you a Merry Christmas," they sang over and over again. Jo looked up at the curtained windows, expecting curious faces to appear, but they didn't.

A team of huskies scampered towards her towing an empty sledge. "Jump in," they barked. Jo did as she was told, wrapping herself in the fleecy blankets that lay on the

seat. The huskies raced off with her to the other side of the green where there was a small playground. Jo was astonished to see a polar bear cub spinning on the roundabout. Another was standing at the top of the slide. "Come on up!" it cried before sliding down on its bottom. Jo jumped out of the sledge and ran up the steps. "Here I come!" she yelled. She slid down head first and fell in a

heap with the cub. She ran across to the roundabout and jumped on next to the other cub. The other children ran over and began to spin them around. Jo gripped the sides of the roundabout as they went faster and faster. Everything became a blur.

When at last they came to a halt, Jo was so tired that she struggled to keep her eyes open. She was helped

from the roundabout by the group of penguins. "Time for bed," they seemed to be saying as they waddled back with her to her house. Before she went inside, Jo looked back at the green. The moonlight was fading. She thought she could just make out the shapes of the snowmen but they seemed to be shrinking and the children had all disappeared. She said goodbye to the penguins, closed the door and crawled back upstairs to bed.

When she woke the next morning, she wondered where she was. And then she remembered that it was Christmas

Day. She jumped out of bed and looked out of the window. The sun was shining brightly. The village green was empty. Jo gazed at it long and hard, half expecting snowmen to appear and a group of penguins to waddle by. She smiled as she remembered the polar bear cub on the slide.

"Still looking for snow?" Her father's voice made her jump.

"It snowed last night but it's all melted," grinned Jo.

Her father shook his head. "You'll be telling me you went sledding next," he chuckled.

"With huskies," Jo laughed. She linked arms with him and said happily, "It's going to be a beautiful Christmas Day, isn't it?"

Jesus Is Born

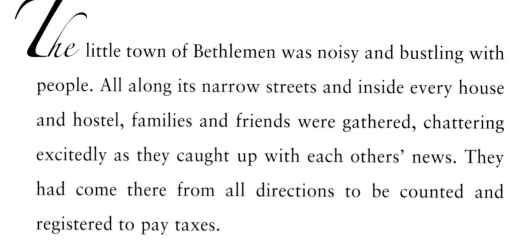

The little town of Bethlemen was noisy and bustling with people. All along its narrow streets and inside every house and hostel, families and friends were gathered, chattering excitedly as they caught up with each others' news. They had come there from all directions to be counted and registered to pay taxes.

A young couple called Joseph and Mary approached the town in the cool of the evening. They had travelled all day from Nazareth, Joseph on foot and Mary on a donkey, and they were both exhausted.

As they plodded along, Mary thought happily of the son she would soon bring into the world and of the messenger from God who had brought her the news. The angel Gabriel had told her that her son would be called Jesus, that he would be known as the Son of God Most High,

and that he would save people from their sins.

As soon as they reached Bethlehem, they began to look for somewhere to stay. They tried one place after another, but met with the same response everywhere they went: "Sorry but we're full." When at last they came to an inn, they were desperate to find somewhere to rest. There were no rooms left there either. The innkeeper shook his head sadly, but when he saw that Mary was expecting a child he took pity on her.

"I'm afraid the only place I can offer you is my stable," he said. "It's not much, I know, but it's clean and warm."

Mary and Joseph smiled gratefully. "You are very kind," they said.

The innkeeper led them round to the back of the inn, across a courtyard to a small building where sheep and oxen were feeding, but where at least there was fresh straw to lie on and shelter from the cold night air. Mary and Joseph thanked him again before he left them to make themselves as comfortable as they could.

In this humble dwelling, Mary gave birth to the baby Jesus. She wrapped him in cloths and made a bed for him in a manger. The sheep and oxen looked on in wonder.

Meanwhile, out in the fields nearby, shepherds were watching over their flocks as they did every night. Some of them talked quietly round a fire, others ambled over the hills on the lookout for thieves and wild animals. All of a sudden, the sky was flooded with dazzling light and an angel of the Lord appeared. The glory of the

Lord shone around the shepherds and they were terrified.

"Do not be afraid," said the angel. "I have come with good news for you and all people. Today, in Bethlehem, a Saviour has been born. He is Christ the Lord. You will find him wrapped in cloths and lying in a manger." Then the heavens opened wide and filled with angels singing, "Glory to God in the highest heaven, and on earth peace to men who follow the path of goodness."

In an instant the angels disappeared and the sky grew dark again. The shepherds still gazed upwards, not daring to speak or move. For many minutes silence enveloped the hillside. Then one of the shepherds said, "Let's go quickly to Bethlehem and see for ourselves this thing that has happened."

They hurried down the path towards the sleeping town. It took them several hours but at last, as dawn broke, they reached the outskirts. They walked quickly along the deserted streets, following the light of the star, until it guided them to the door of a stable. "Can it really be here?" they asked each other. They peered inside. What they saw filled their hearts with great joy and wonderment. A tiny baby lay in a manger, just as the angel had told them. Mary sat close by stroking his hand, with Joseph at her side and sheep and oxen bleating and braying all around. The shepherds threw themselves to the ground in adoration.

When daylight came to Bethlehem, the shepherds bade farewell to Mary and Joseph rushed out on to the streets. Wherever they went they told people about the birth of the baby Jesus and what they had seen and heard. The news spread fast, not just across the town but across the world. Before very long there was great rejoicing everywhere.

The Christmas Mouse

*W*hen all was quiet on Christmas Eve, a mouse crept out from a hole in the wall and pattered along the carpet in the hall and FROZE. It wasn't because she had seen a cat. It wasn't because she had seen a human. What she had seen was a tree! The mouse – Ruby she called herself – rubbed her eyes and waggled her whiskers, but when she looked again the tree was still there. "I'm sure that tree is where a tree shouldn't be," she muttered

to herself. "And it certainly wasn't there last time I went for a walk."

She tiptoed towards it, tiny step by tiny step, then stopped. "I might be a house mouse," she said, "but even I can tell that that tree is covered with the strangest flowers." She scampered a little closer until she was standing right underneath one of the flowers. She looked up. What she saw nearly made her faint with shock. There was a mouse inside the flower!

"Hello," said Ruby at last, when she had recovered from her shock.

The mouse seemed to say hello at the same time, and moved its head when Ruby moved her head. Feeling bolder, Ruby stood on her hind legs to rub noses with the stranger. Its nose was as cold and as hard as ice. When she held up her paw, the other mouse held up its paw as well, but when Ruby tried to touch it the flower swung backwards, taking the mouse with it.

"Don't go," Ruby cried, but the mouse

seemed to have disappeared when she looked at the flower again. Ruby decided that it was very unfriendly, and besides she wanted to carry on exploring.

Piled underneath the tree were lots of odd-shaped objects covered in coloured paper. "That paper would look nice in my nest," Ruby thought to herself. She began to chew at the corners of one of the shapes. As she tugged at it, the paper came away and a furry leg sprang up. Ruby squealed with fright and hid under a chair. She stared out, expecting the leg to start moving. When it didn't, she crept slowly towards it until she was right up close, then poked it. Still nothing happened. Carefully she pulled away the rest of the paper. A face appeared, which made her run away again, but then she realised that it was a bear. Ruby had seen bears before, on human beds. Humans liked to cuddle them, but they were harmless to mice. "Silly things," she muttered to herself. "What's the point of a furry animal that can't move?"

Ruby was feeling hungry now. She knew that food was kept in another room, but on her way there she discovered a plate of crumbs and sugar, and next to it a half-eaten carrot. They were right by the place where humans sometimes threw bits of trees and burned them to make themselves hot. (That was the only time Ruby had seen trees in the house before.) She sniffed at the crumbs and sugar to check that they were all right to eat, then she took a little mouthful. "Mmm," she said. "Delicious. I wonder if they were left there specially for me." She took a big bite of carrot and crunched on it happily. "This is a good night for me," she said to herself. "Those humans must have decided they like having me around."

When she had finished eating, Ruby set off across the room again. She had spotted something unusual on a low

table. It was a tiny house with sheep and cows standing outside it. Ruby leapt up on to the table and poked her nose at one of the sheep, which was about the same size as she was. It fell over. She pushed past a donkey, which fell over as well, and pattered into the house. A man and a woman were sitting there. Another tiny human was lying down in a funny sort of bed. Even Ruby could tell that the people and the animals weren't real, but she wondered what they were doing there and why the house was full of straw. And then she thought to herself, "It must be for me. They've given me my own little house and my own bed of straw, and they've made it feel like home by giving me people and animals to watch over me."

Ruby was overjoyed. "This is the best night of my life," she chuckled. She sniffed at the straw and sat down in it. "Very comfortable," she said. She washed her feet and preened her whiskers. "I don't know who the tree is for, but my new home is perfect." She curled up in a ball, tucked her nose into her paws, and soon she was fast asleep and snoring gently.

Christmas Cookies

INGREDIENTS
1½ cups butter, softened
2 cups granulated sugar
4 eggs
1 teaspoon vanilla extract
5 cups all-purpose flour
2 teaspoons baking powder
1 teaspoon salt

MAKES 5 dozen

DIRECTIONS
FOR THE COOKIES:

1. In a large bowl, cream together butter and sugar until smooth.

2. Beat in eggs and vanilla. Stir in the flour, baking powder and salt.

3. Cover and chill dough for at least one hour (or overnight).

4. Preheat oven to 400° F.

ICING
4 cups confectioners' sugar
½ cup shortening
5 tablespoons milk
1 teaspoon vanilla extract
Food coloring (optional)

5. Roll out dough ¼ to ½ inch thick on a floured surface and cut into shapes with cookie cutters.

6. Place cookies 1 inch apart on ungreased cookie sheets.

7. Bake 6 to 8 minutes in preheated oven. Cool completely.

FOR THE ICING:

1. In a large bowl, cream together the confectioners' sugar and shortening with an electric mixer until smooth.

2. Gradually mix in the milk and vanilla until smooth and stiff, about 5 minutes.

3. Color with food coloring if desired.

4. To make your cookies even prettier, add sugar balls, stars and sprinkles.

The Twelve Days of Christmas

On the first day of Christmas my true love gave to me – a partridge in a pear tree!

On the second day of Christmas my true love gave to me – two turtle doves and a partridge in a pear tree!

On the third day of Christmas my true love gave to me – three French hens, two turtle doves and a partridge in a pear tree!

On the fourth day of Christmas my true love gave to me – four calling birds, three French hens, two turtle doves and a partridge in a pear tree!

On the fifth day of Christmas my true love gave to me – five golden rings, four calling birds, three French hens, two turtle doves and a partridge in a pear tree!

On the sixth day of Christmas

my true love gave to me – six geese a layin', five golden rings, four calling birds, three French hens, two turtle doves and a partridge in a pear tree!

On the seventh day of

Christmas my true love gave to me – seven swans a swimmin', six geese a layin', five golden rings, four calling birds, three French hens, two turtle doves and a partridge in a pear tree!

On the eighth day of Christmas my

true love gave to me – eight maids a milkin', seven swans a swimmin', six geese a layin', five golden rings, four calling birds, three French hens, two turtle doves and a partridge in a pear tree!

On the ninth day of Christmas my

true love gave to me – nine pipers pipin', eight maids a milkin', seven swans a swimmin', six geese a layin', five golden rings, four calling birds, three French hens, two turtle doves and a partridge in a pear tree!

On the tenth day of Christmas my true love gave to me – ten ladies dancin', nine pipers pipin', eight maids a milkin', seven swans a swimmin', six geese a layin', five golden rings, four calling birds, three French hens, two turtle doves and a partridge in a pear tree!

On the eleventh day of Christmas my true love gave to me – eleven lords a leapin', ten ladies dancin', nine pipers pipin', eight maids a milkin', seven swans a swimmin', six geese a layin', five golden rings, four calling birds, three French hens, two turtle doves and a partridge in a pear tree!

On the twelfth day of Christmas my true love gave to me – twelve drummers drummin', eleven lords a leapin', ten ladies dancin', nine pipers pipin', eight maids a milkin', seven swans a swimmin', six geese a layin', five golden rings, four calling birds, three French hens, two turtle doves and a partridge in a pear tree!